Words of
FRIENDSHIP

JAKE BIGGIN

These Words of Friendship belong to:

It isn't always easy to find a friend — or to be one.
Words of Friendship has little thoughts
about big questions.
Sunny is always there for Alice.
He accepts who she is,
even when she finds it hard to accept herself.
He helps her to find her way when she feels lost.
Together they discover that friendship is a feeling in your heart…
…and that it's really just another word for love.

Jake

What do you need, Alice?

It doesn't matter, Sunny.

It matters.
You matter.

You can talk to me.
We're friends.

Why do we even need friends?

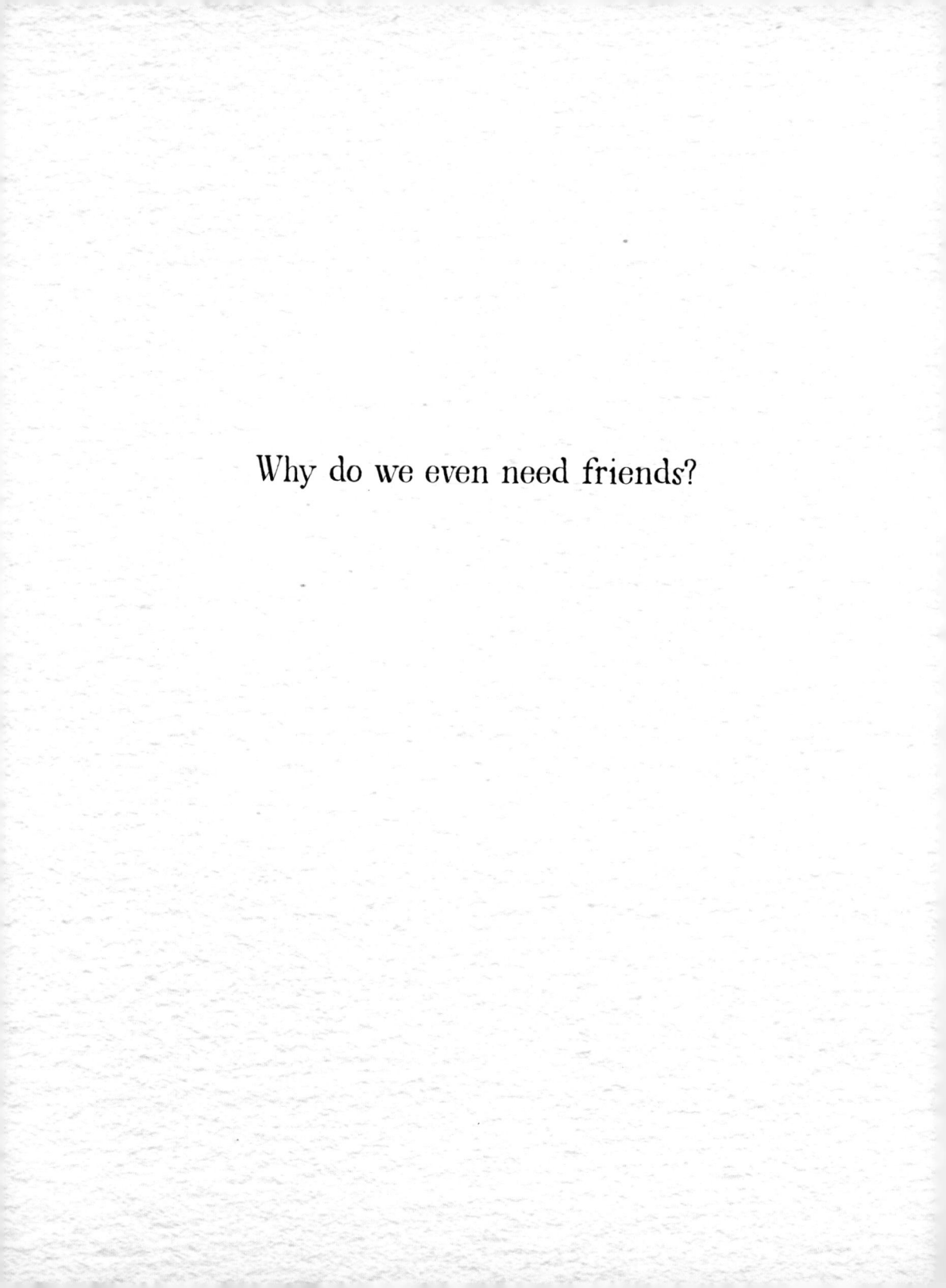

I don't know where to start.

Trust the magic of beginnings.

It's a lovely day. Shall we go for a walk
and think about things together?

What's the best way to get a friend?

To be one.

...and who you will become.

Big feelings just mean you have a big heart.

Feelings are like clouds.

They change and shift.

They aren't forever.

Be kind to yourself
in what you say and what you do.

What should I believe in?

Yourself.

Nobody is always happy.
But looking for one beautiful
thing every day can help.

You don't always have to follow
the thoughts in your head.

Be led by the dreams in your heart.

Just be you.

But who am I?

You are you.
Always be yourself.

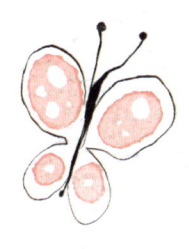

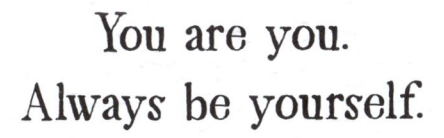

What's the difference between anything and nothing?

I think that almost nothing is certain,
but almost anything is possible.

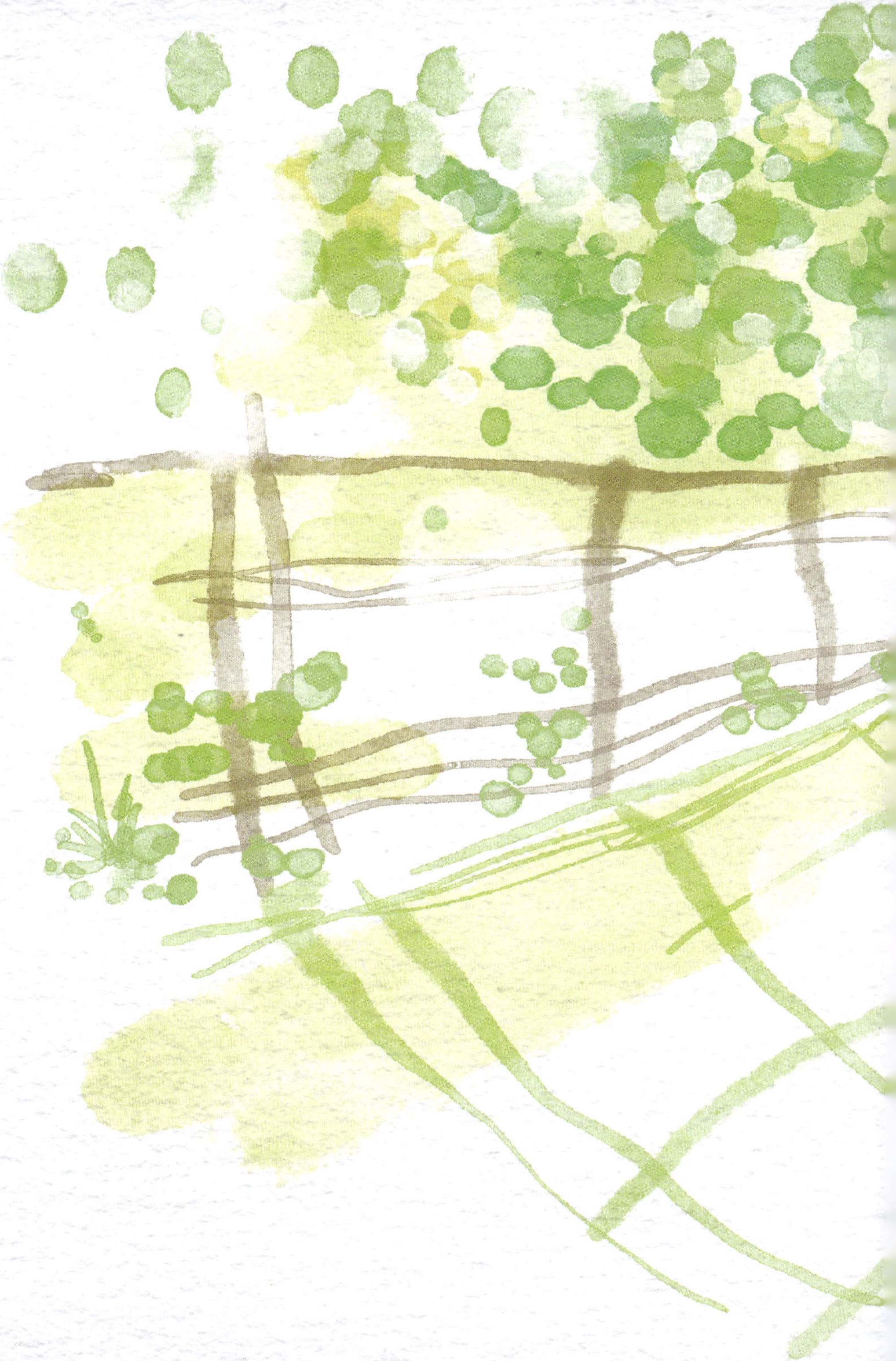

Can I do anything?

The only way you'll
know is if you try.

I don't always have answers
to my questions.

That's OK.
Not all questions have answers.

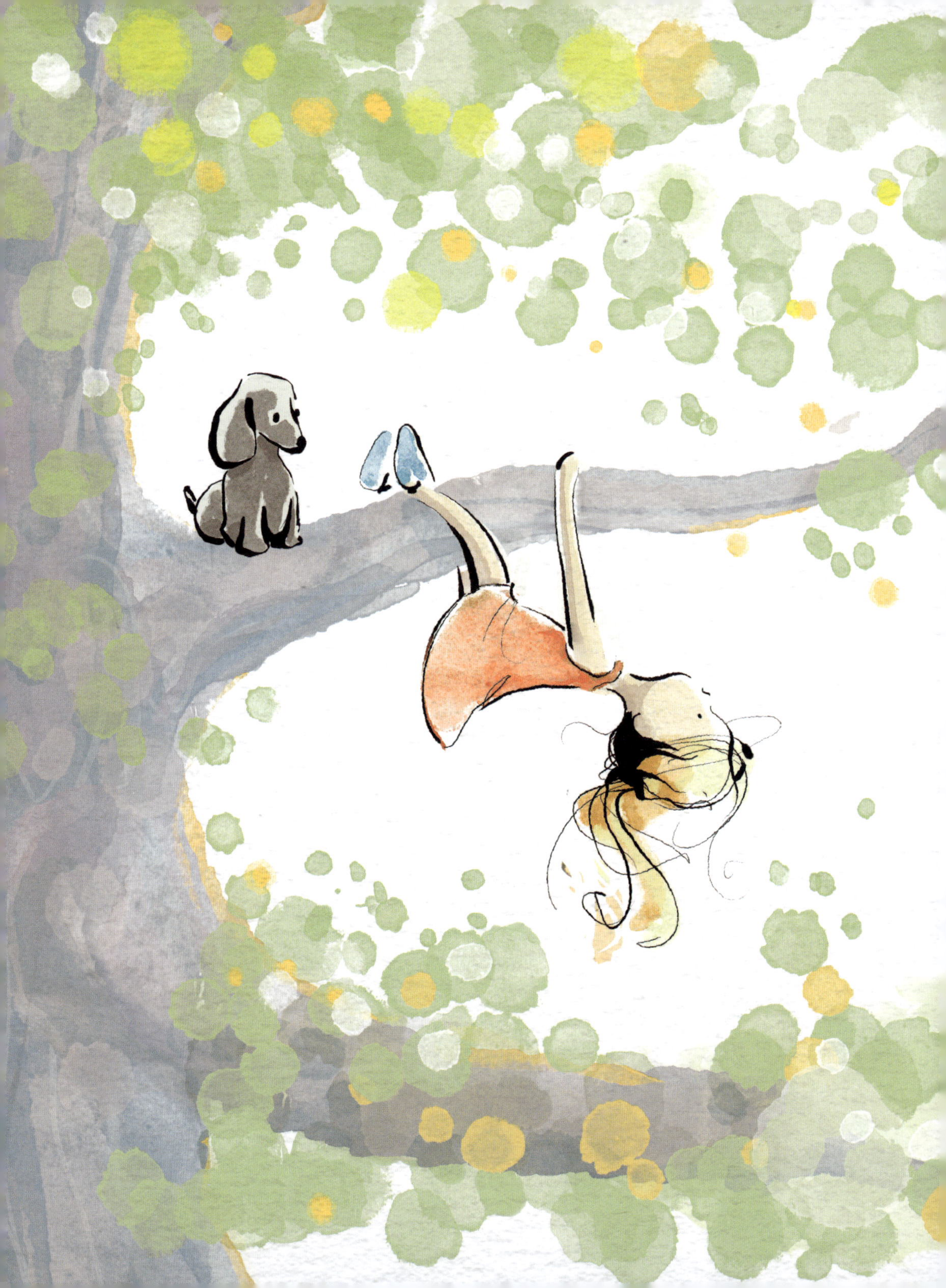

Sometimes, looking at things in a new way lets you see more.

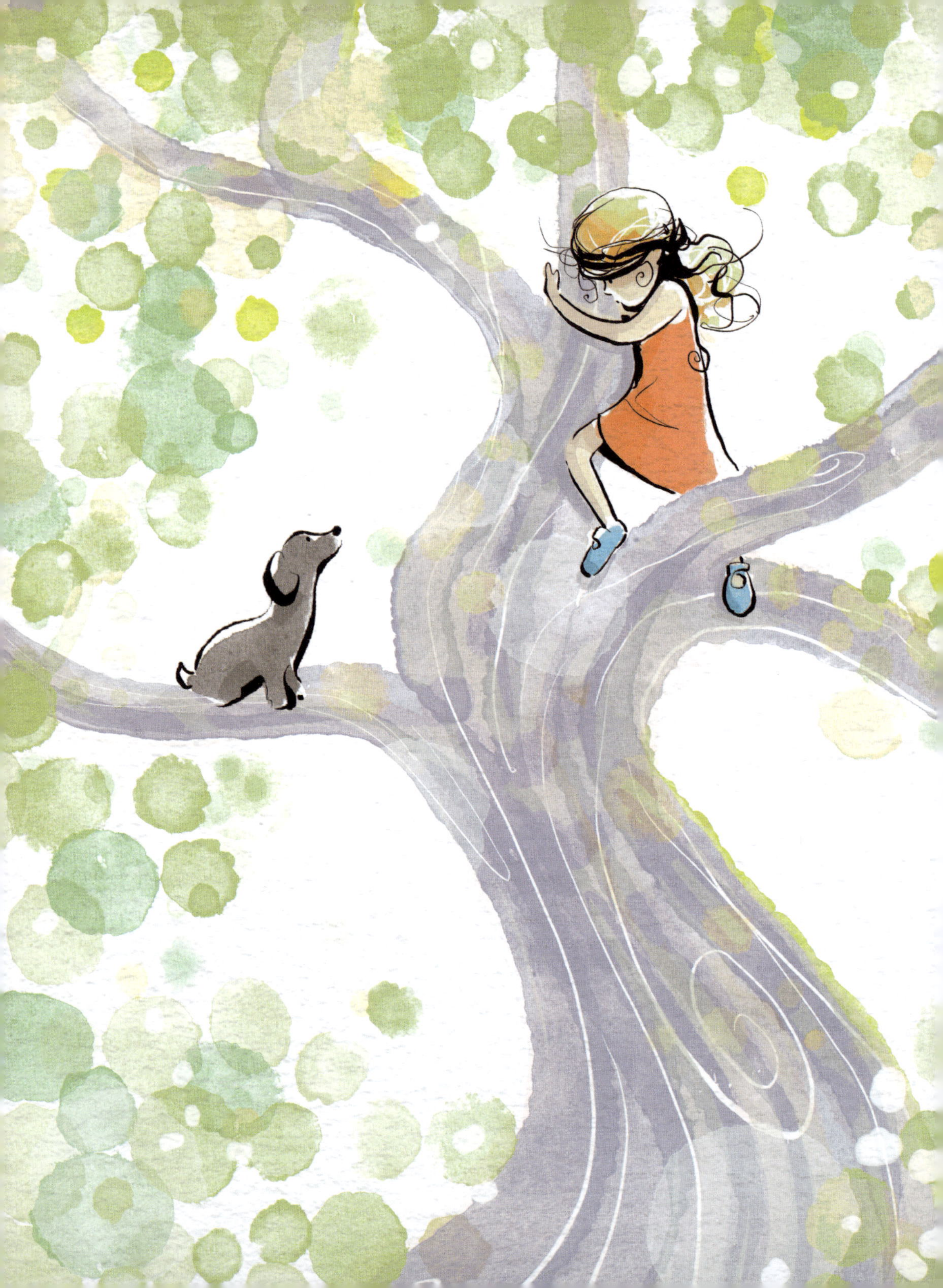

You can reach out to me.

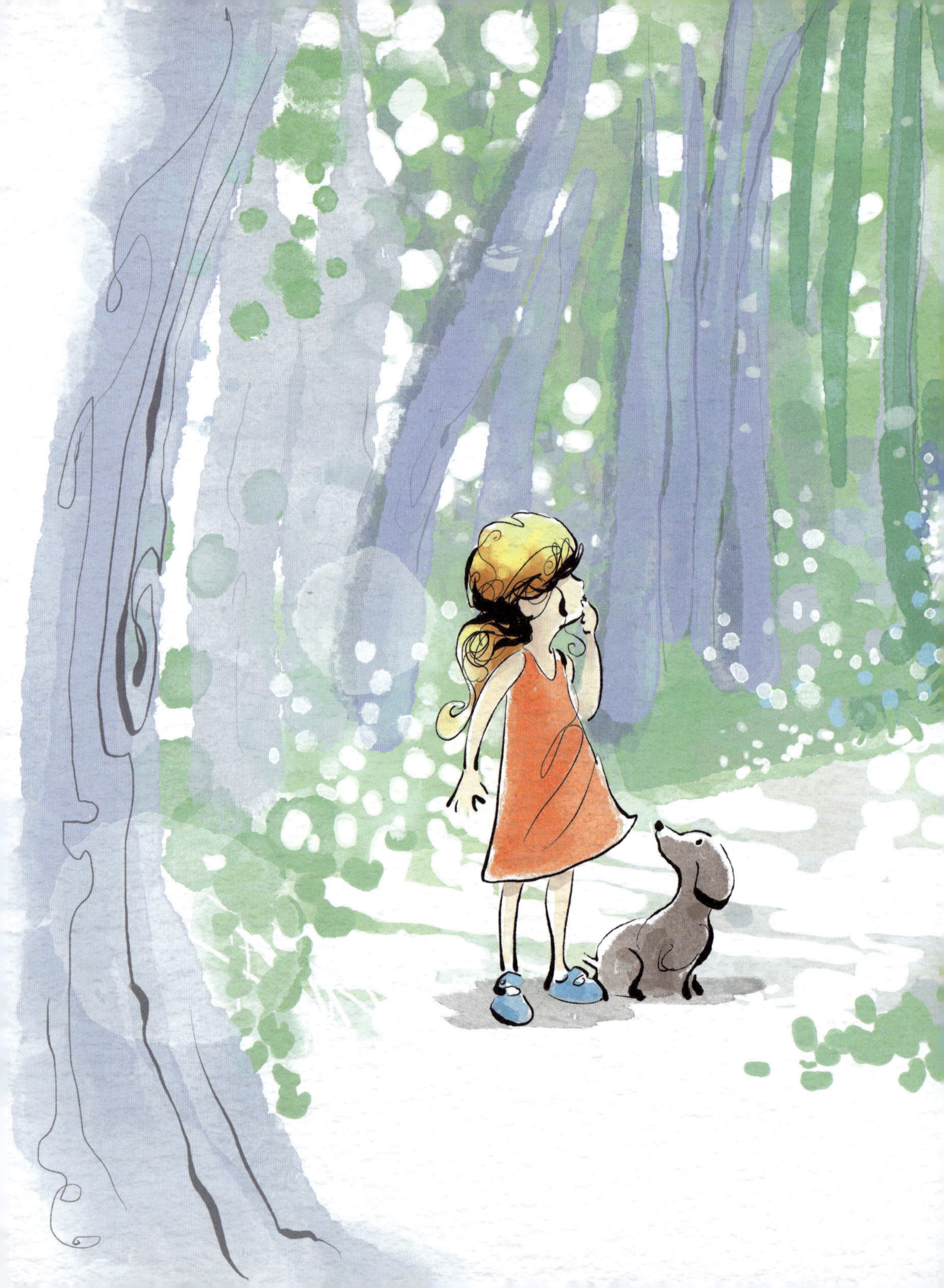

Follow your heart.
It knows the way.

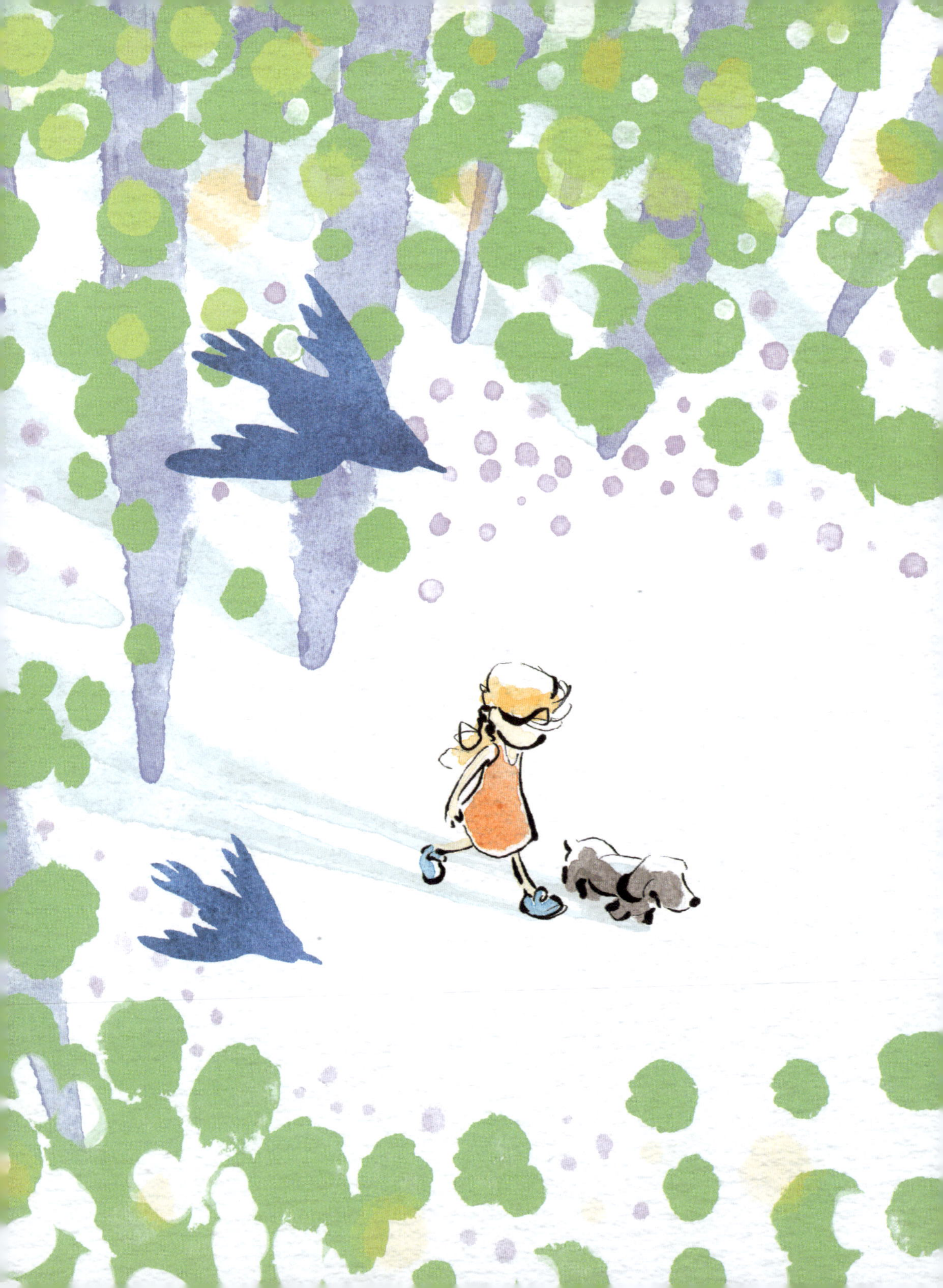

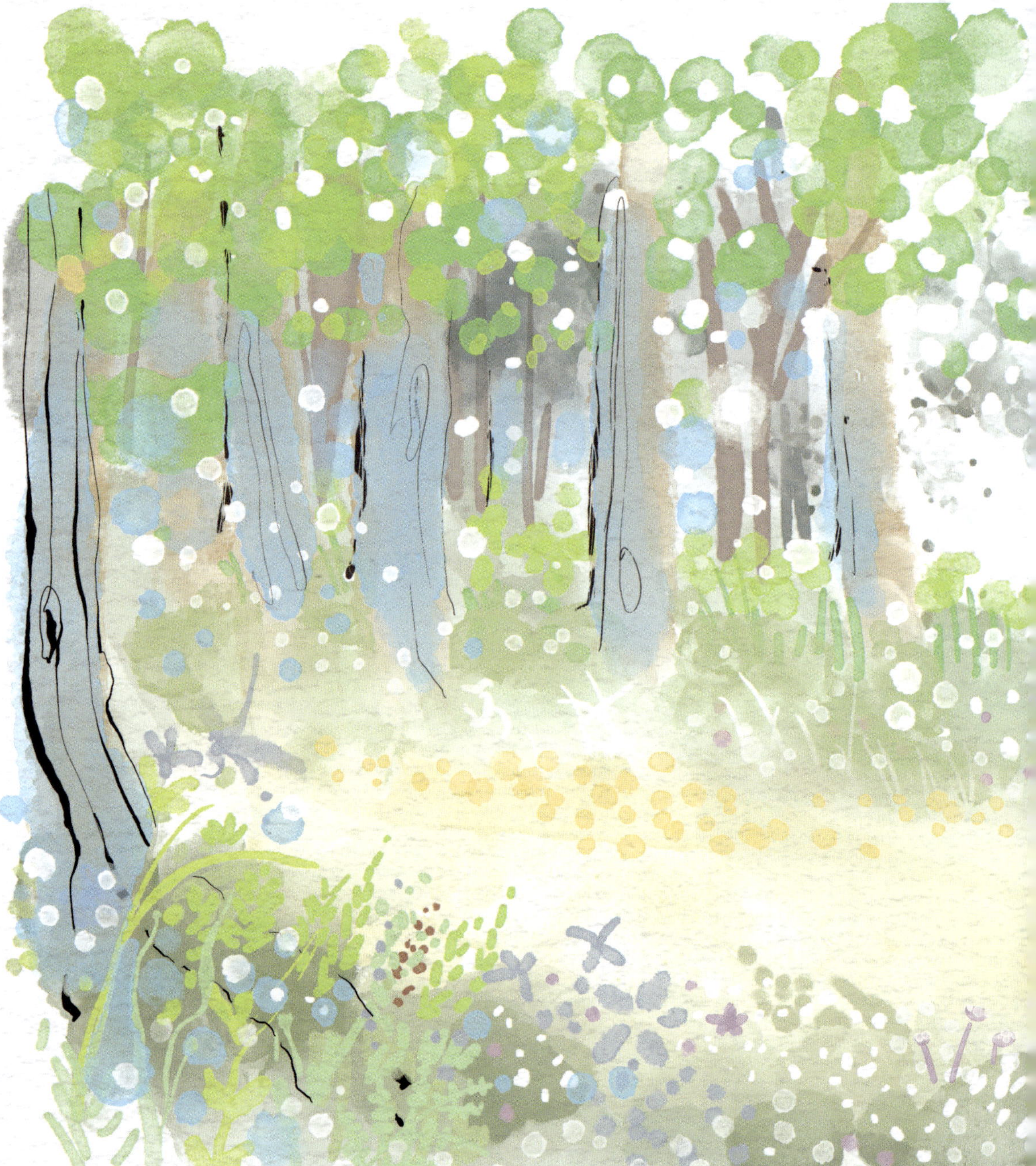

You're my best friend,
Sunny.

You help me to feel happy.

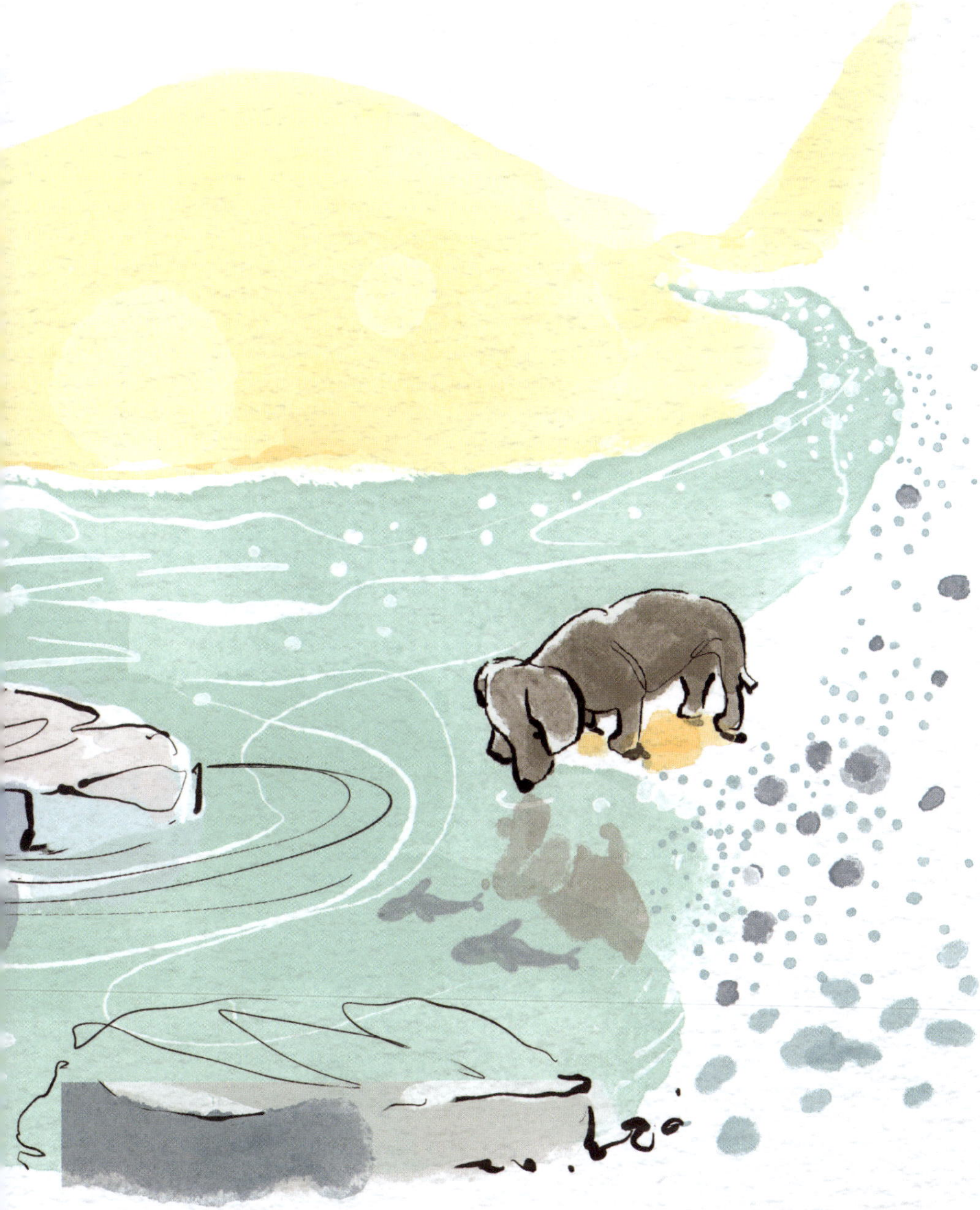

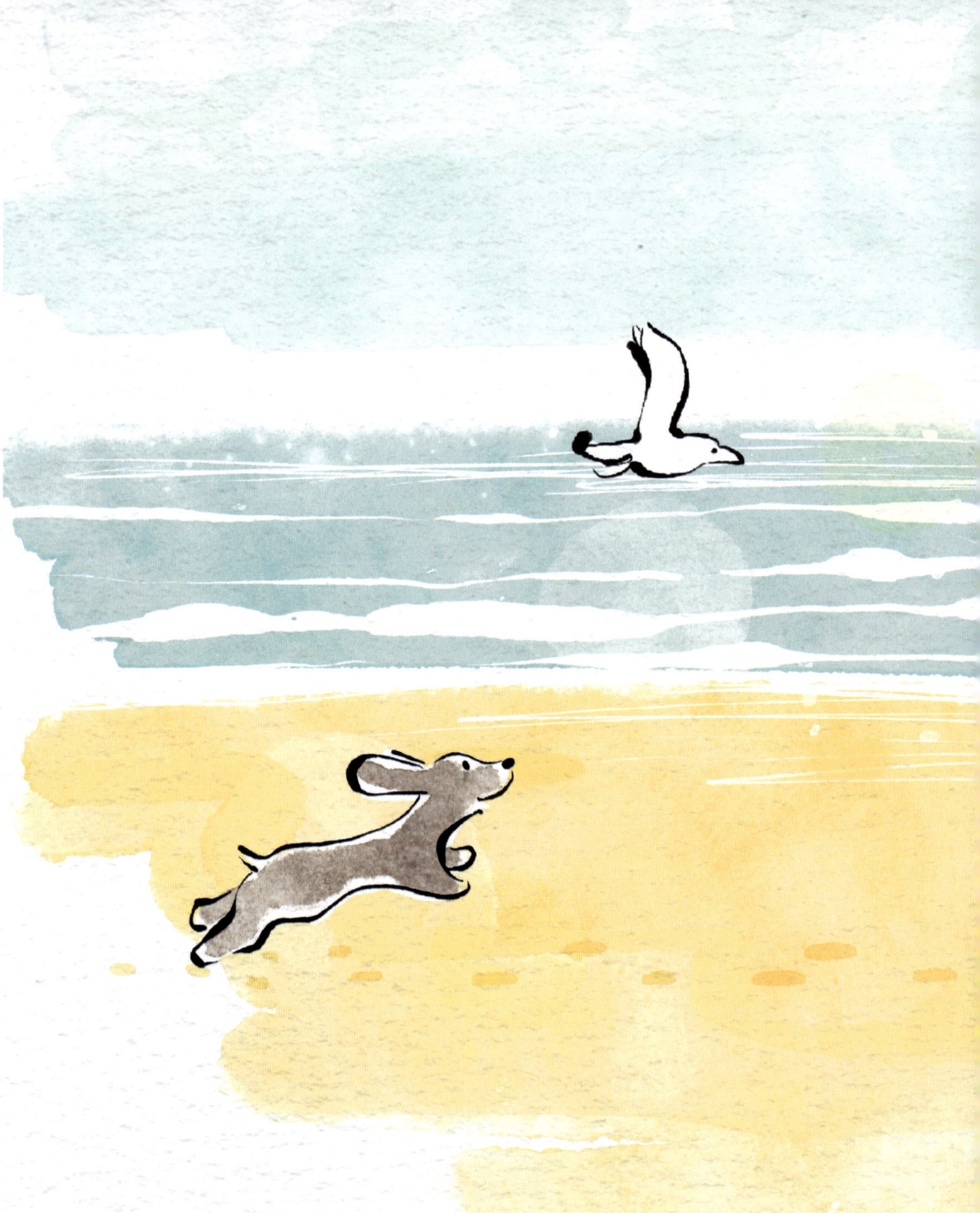

With you, I can be myself.

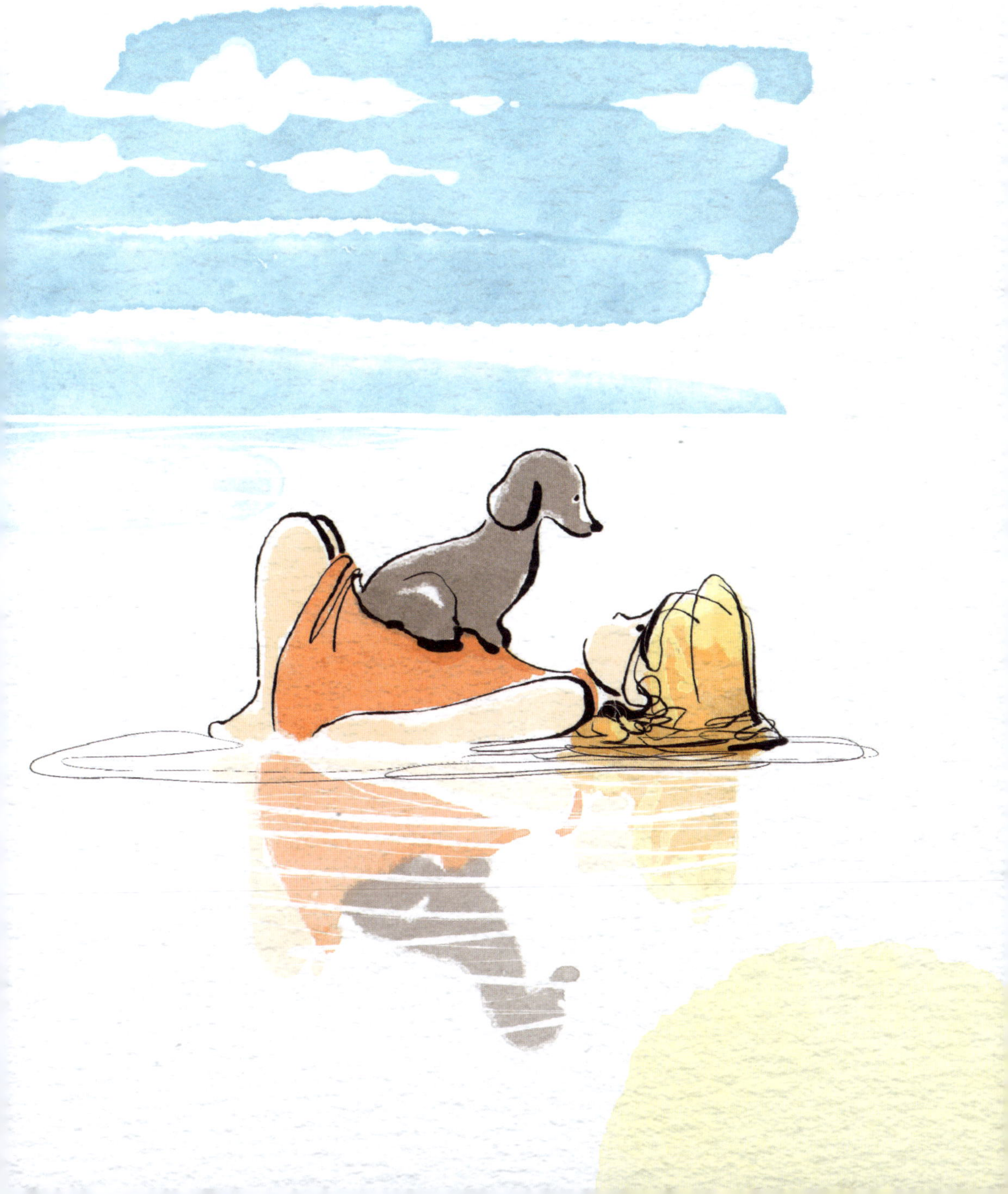

I found my one
beautiful thing today.

What is it?

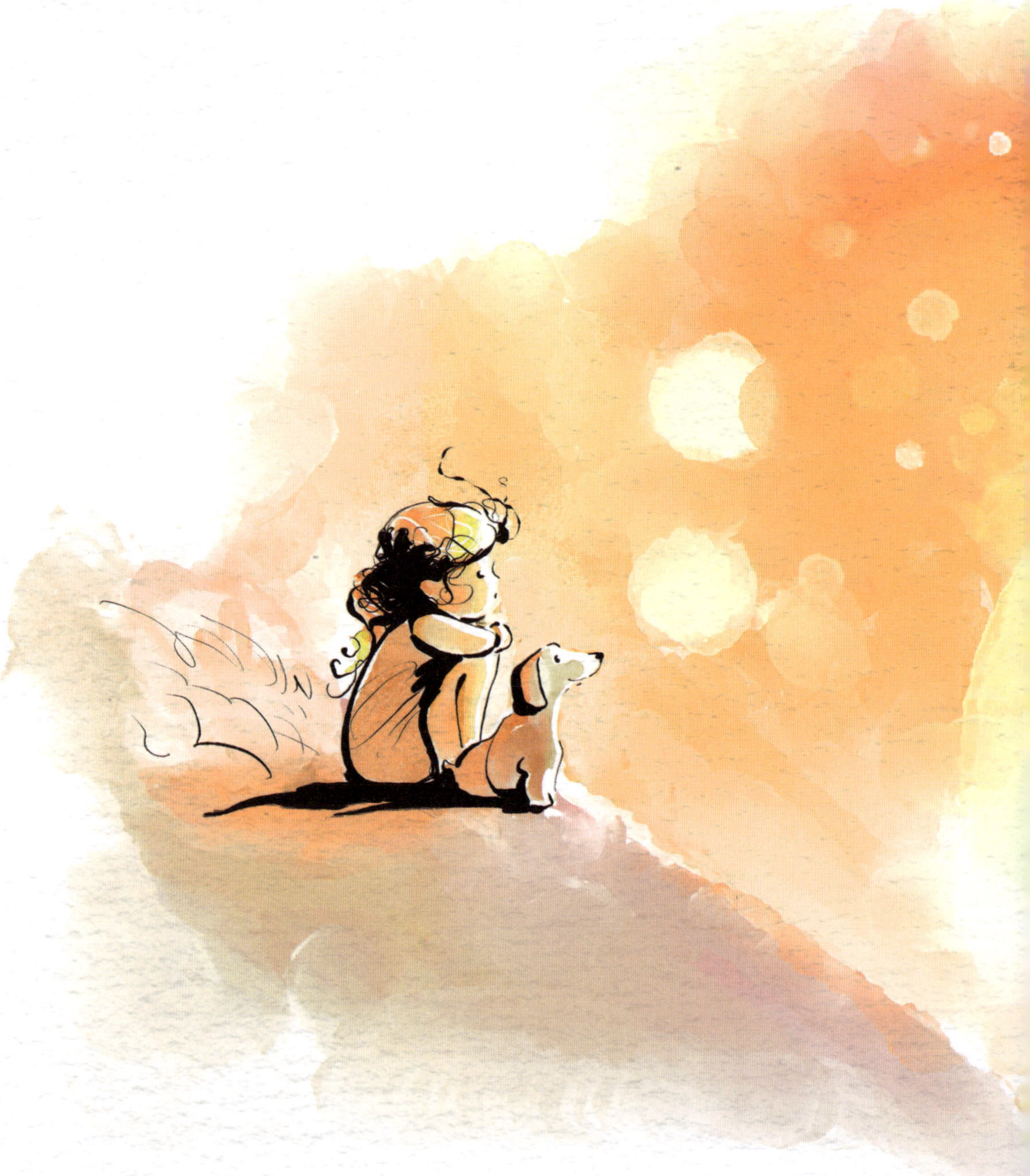

Us.

Author and Illustrator Jake Biggin

Editor Rona Skene
Designer Ella Tomkins
Additional Editorial Becca Arlington
Additional Design Vic Palastanga
Production Editor Becky Fallowfield
Senior Production Controller Ben Radley
Jacket Coordinator Elin Woosnam
Managing Art Editor Anna Hall
Art Director Mabel Chan
Associate Publishing Director Francesca Young

First published in Great Britain in 2025 by
Dorling Kindersley Limited
20 Vauxhall Bridge Road,
London SW1V 2SA

The authorised representative in the EEA is
Dorling Kindersley Verlag GmbH. Arnulfstr. 124,
80636 Munich, Germany

Text and illustration copyright © Jake Biggin 2025
Jake Biggin has asserted his right to be identified
as the author and illustrator of this work
Layout and design copyright © 2025
Dorling Kindersley Limited

A Penguin Random House Company
10 9 8 7 6 5 4 3 2 1
001–351156–Nov/2025

All rights reserved.
No part of this publication may be reproduced, stored in or introduced into a retrieval system, or transmitted, in any form, or by any means (electronic, mechanical, photocopying, recording, or otherwise), without the prior written permission of the copyright owner.

DK values and supports copyright. Thank you for respecting intellectual property laws by not reproducing, scanning or distributing any part of this publication by any means without permission. By purchasing an authorised edition, you are supporting writers and artists and enabling DK to continue to publish books that inform and inspire readers. No part of this publication may be used or reproduced in any manner for the purpose of training artificial intelligence technologies or systems. In accordance with Article 4(3) of the DSM Directive 2019/790, DK expressly reserves this work from the text and data mining exception.

A CIP catalogue record for this book
is available from the British Library.
ISBN: 978-0-2417-6063-5

Printed and bound in China

www.dk.com

This book was made with Forest Stewardship Council™ certified paper – one small step in DK's commitment to a sustainable future. Learn more at www.dk.com/uk/information/sustainability

For Sam, Alice, and all our friends

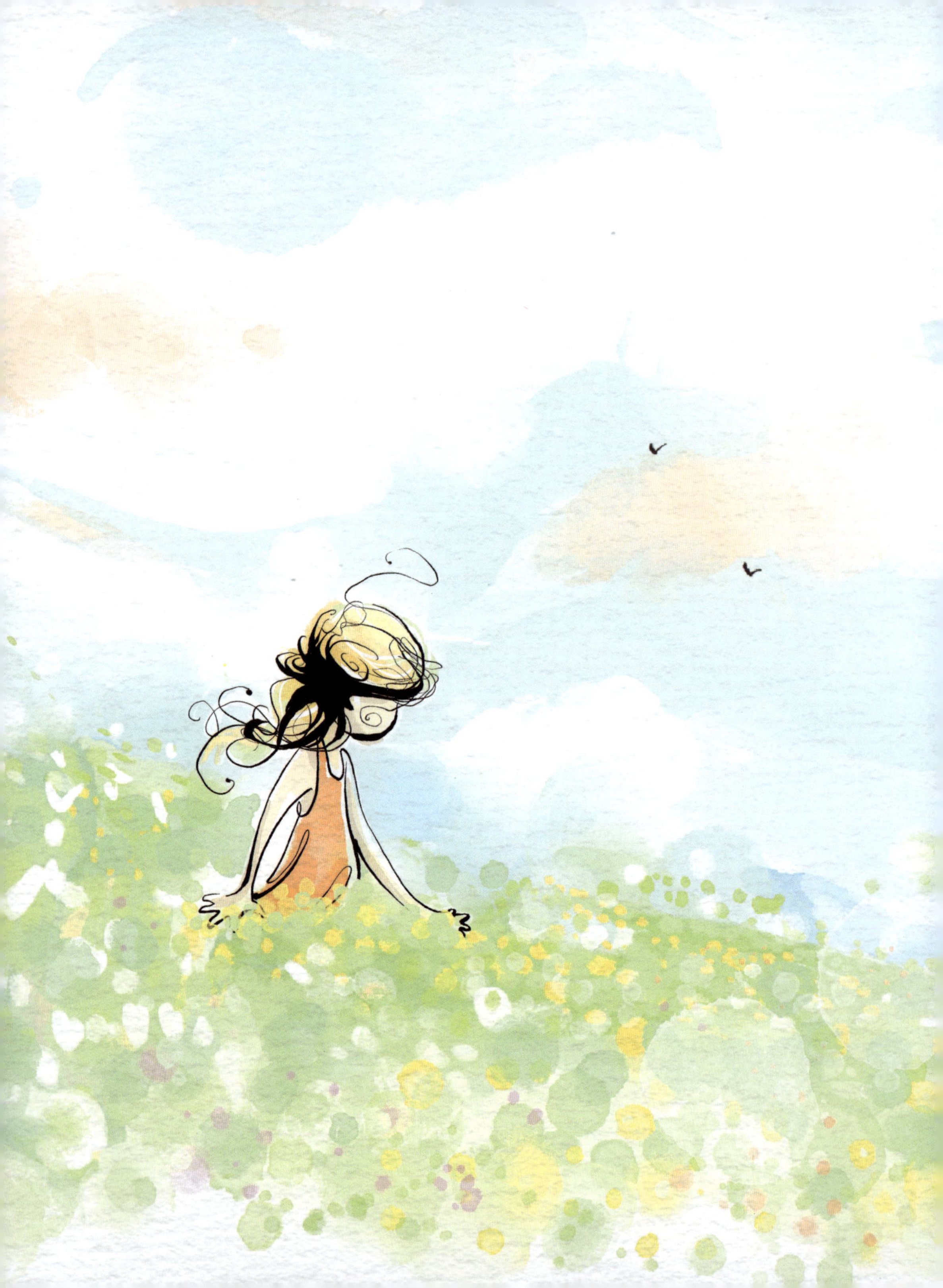